—For mothers and children everywhere
—A.R.

For Mom
—L.R.

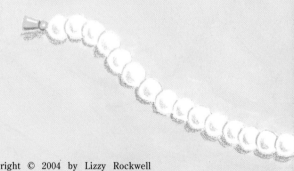

Mother's Day   Text copyright © 2004 by Anne Rockwell   Illustrations copyright © 2004 by Lizzy Rockwell
Manufactured in China by South China Printing Company Ltd. All rights reserved.   www.harperchildrens.com   Library of Congress
Cataloging-in-Publication Data   Rockwell, Anne F.   Mother's Day / story by Anne Rockwell ; pictures by Lizzy Rockwell. — 1st ed.
p.   cm.   Summary: The students in Mrs. Madoff's class share how they will celebrate Mother's Day with their families.
ISBN 0-06-051374-8 — ISBN 0-06-051375-6 (lib. bdg.)   [1. Mother's Day—Fiction. 2. Schools—Fiction.] I. Rockwell, Lizzy, ill. II.
Title. PZ7.R5943Mq 2004 [E]—dc21 2003000444 Typography by Elynn Cohen   1 2 3 4 5 6 7 8 9 10 ❖ First Edition

Mother's Day

ANNE ROCKWELL   pictures by LIZZY ROCKWELL

HARPERCOLLINSPUBLISHERS

"Eveline, what are you going to do
at school today?" Maman asked me.
"I can't tell you," I said. "That's a secret!"

At school, Nicholas and I walked
down the hall together.
He said, "Hey, Eveline!
Did you remember to bring one?"
I nodded and showed him
my shiny gold button.
"Mine's yellow with red stripes," he said.

At circle time, Mrs. Madoff said,
"What holiday will we celebrate
this Sunday?"
"MOTHER'S DAY!" we shouted.

"Good. Did everyone remember to
bring a button?" she asked.
Everyone had.
"Eveline, how will your family celebrate
Mother's Day?" asked Mrs. Madoff.

"My maman will be very happy!" I said.
"My big brother will come home from college.
He and Papa will make beignets
and I'll roll them in powdered sugar.
We won't let Maman help because
Sunday is her special day."

"Mom and I are hiking to the top
of Chickasaw Mountain," said Jessica.
"Just the two of us.
She loves to hike, and so do I.
I bought the kind of sweet, fat, black
seedless grapes she loves for our picnic."

"Dad and I are going to give Mom
the birdhouse we built.
It has a tiny hole," Evan said.
"The hole is tiny so that
only wrens can fly in or out.
Wrens are the cutest birds in our yard.
That's what Mom says."

"My mother died when I was a baby," Sarah said.
"Dad and I live with Grandma, who's his mother.
She does everything for me that mothers do.

On Mother's Day, Dad and I will
take her to a restaurant that has
the kind of food her mom cooked.

Pablo said, "Last week,
my father was bulldozing.
Suddenly he saw a little dogwood tree.
He stopped his bulldozer just in time.
He dug it up, roots and all,
and put it in our garage.
On Mother's Day we'll plant it
in our yard!
That little dogwood tree sure will
make my mother happy!"

"We're not doing anything for Momma
on Mother's Day," said Charlie.
"Instead she is throwing a baby shower
for her twin sister, Aunt Louisa.

My aunt is going to have a baby.
Then she'll be a mother to her baby
like Momma is to me!
Dad says Momma sure is nice to share
her special day with Aunt Louisa."

Kate said, "Daddy's been teaching me
to play the violin while Mommy's at work.
I can play the piece I learned for you."
Kate tucked the violin under her chin,
picked up the bow, and played.
"I practice my piece every day,"
she said, as soon as we'd finished clapping.
"I want to play it perfectly on Mother's Day!"

Michiko said, "My mother is tired of
only looking at pictures she draws.

So my father and I decided the best gift
we could give her was an all-day trip to
the biggest museum in the city."

"On Mother's Day, we're going shopping
at the mall for a new kitchen table.
I took all the money out of
my piggy bank," Sam said.
"It will help us buy my mother
a new table with chairs to match."

"Don't forget me!" said Nicholas.
"You know I never would!" Mrs. Madoff said.
"My mom loves animals, but all
we have is a goldfish.
You know what? She's getting a puppy
for Mother's Day! I picked him out."

Mrs. Madoff said it was time
to make Mother's Day presents.

A lady I never saw before came
into our classroom.
"Boys and girls," said Mrs. Madoff.
"Here's Annie! She's my mom.
She's going to show us how to make
paper flowers with our buttons."

We started with a circle
of construction paper.

Next we cut petals from
tissue paper and glued
them all around the circle.
That made a flower.

Then we glued
our buttons in
the center of
each tissue-
paper flower.

Finally we cut out leaves.
We glued them to fuzzy
pipe cleaners.

When we glued the pipe cleaners to the
flowers, our flowers had leaves and stems!

My pink and red rose with its shiny gold center was the most beautiful thing in the world!

That's what Maman said.

She loved that rose and the beignets
that I brought to her on Mother's Day.